Dreamland

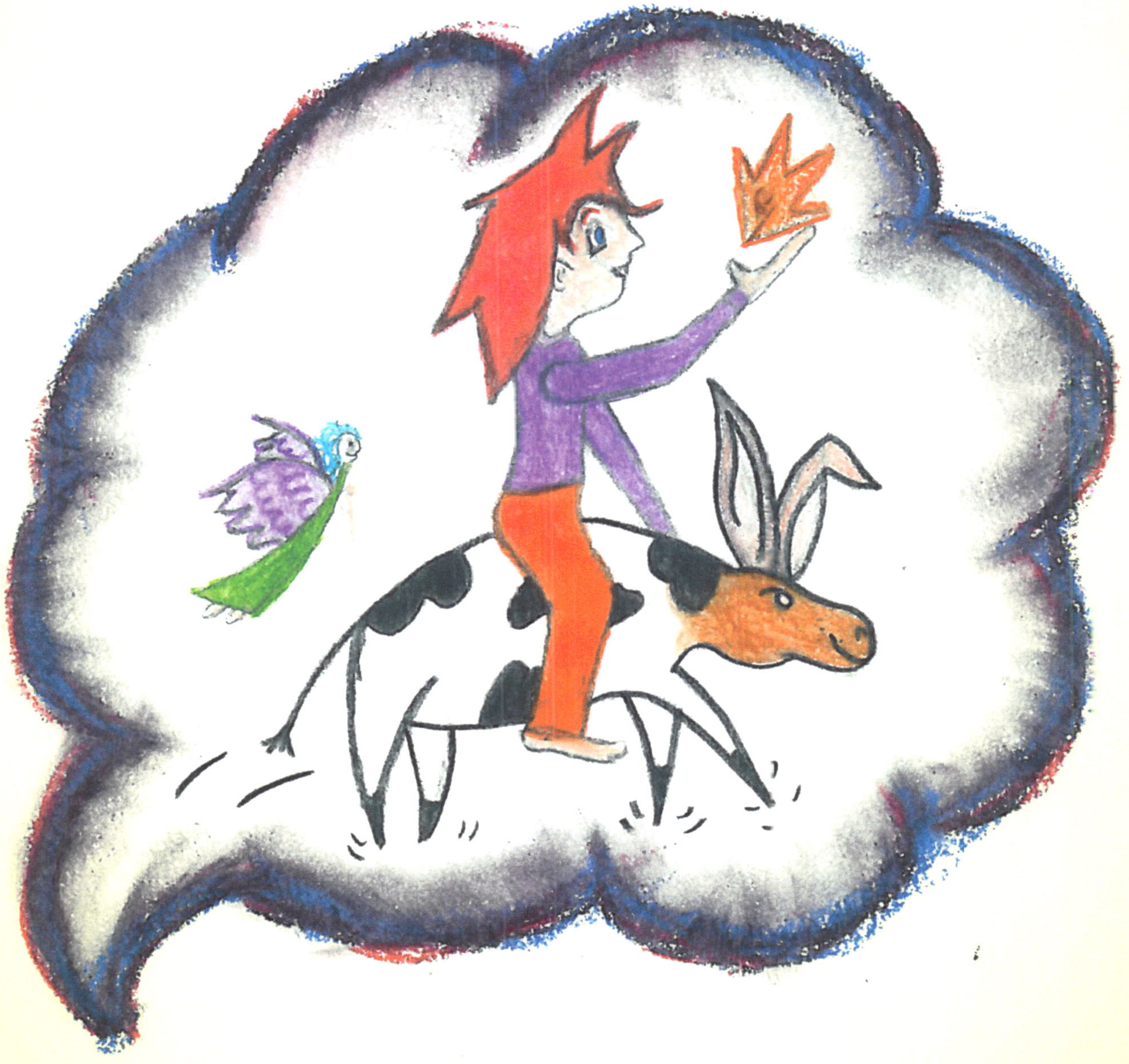

Joshua Walter

Copyright © Joshua Walter.

All rights reserved. No part of this book may be reproduced in any form or by any electronic or mechanical means, including information storage and retrieval systems, without permission in writing from the publisher, except by reviewers, who may quote brief passages in a review.

ISBN: 978-1-64921-238-2 (Paperback Edition)
ISBN: 978-1-64921-239-9 (Hardcover Edition)
ISBN: 978-1-64921-237-5 (E-book Edition)

Some characters and events in this book are fictitious. Any similarity to real persons, living or dead, is coincidental and not intended by the author.

Book Ordering Information

Phone Number: 347-901-4929 or 347-901-4920
Email: info@globalsummithouse.com
Global Summit House
www.globalsummithouse.com

Printed in the United States of America

Its that time again to go to bed,
Sleep my child, rest your little head.
Off to Dreamland you go right now.
Where you can dream what your mind does allow.

Dreamland is the place to be
to escape the worries of reality
Where you can see what you want to see
And be whatever you want to be

You want to be strong, you want to be smart
This is the place where it all does start

Walk on water, fly really high
You can even fly beyond the sky

to outter space if you do so wish
catch a shooting star as if it were a fish.

**Unicorns, Super Heroes, Friends galore
in dreamland there is so much more**

Angels are here to guide the way
Every single night and day

But when you awaken do not despair
As you will be back when nightime reapears

Tomorrow you will be back after your fed
And back to Dreamland, in your bed

www.ingramcontent.com/pod-product-compliance
Lightning Source LLC
LaVergne TN
LVHW071654060526
838200LV00029B/459